Word Fun

priddy books

big ideas for little people

Word jumble

Using the word and picture clues, can you figure out what the four mixed-up words are? Write your answers in the spaces below.

   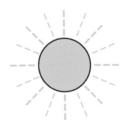

A red flower   _ _ _ _ _   sero

On a tree   _ _ _ _ _   elfa

A slimy bug   _ _ _ _ _ _   nsial

In the sky   _ _ _ _   nsu

Missing letters
Fill in the missing letters of these words.

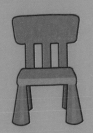   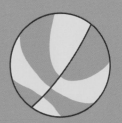

_ hair du _ k bo _ k bal _

Which object would you play with outside?

My body

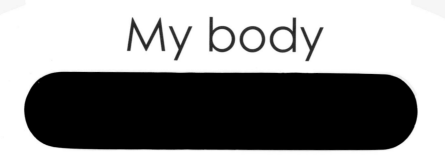

Fill in the missing letters to label the different parts of the body.

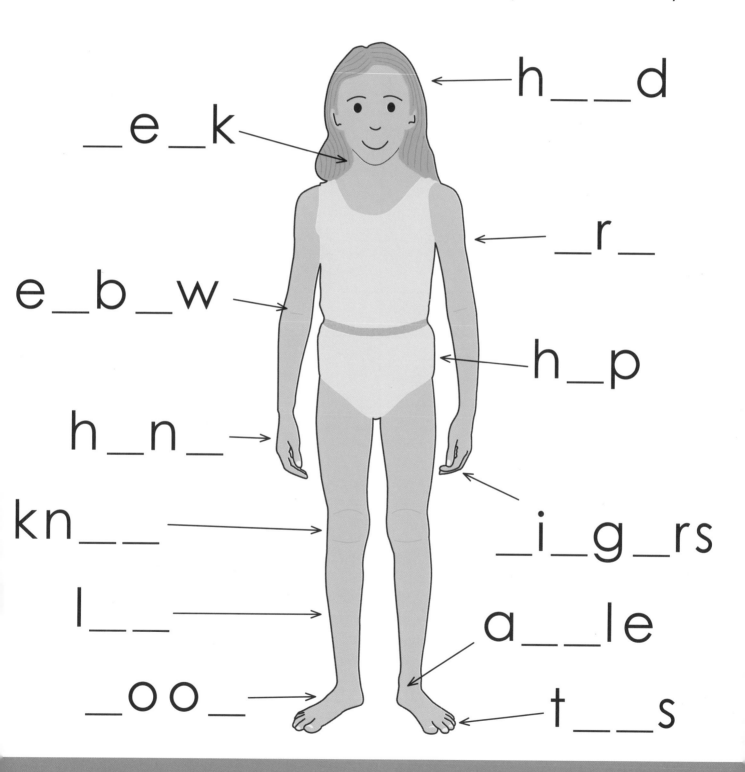

h _ _ d

_ e _ k

_ r _

e _ b _ w

h _ p

h _ n _

kn _ _

_ i _ g _ rs

l _ _

a _ _ le

_ o o _

t _ _ s

How many fingers and toes do you have?

Word wheel

Fill in the missing letters of the shape words on the wheel.
Use these letters to spell the name of the shape below.

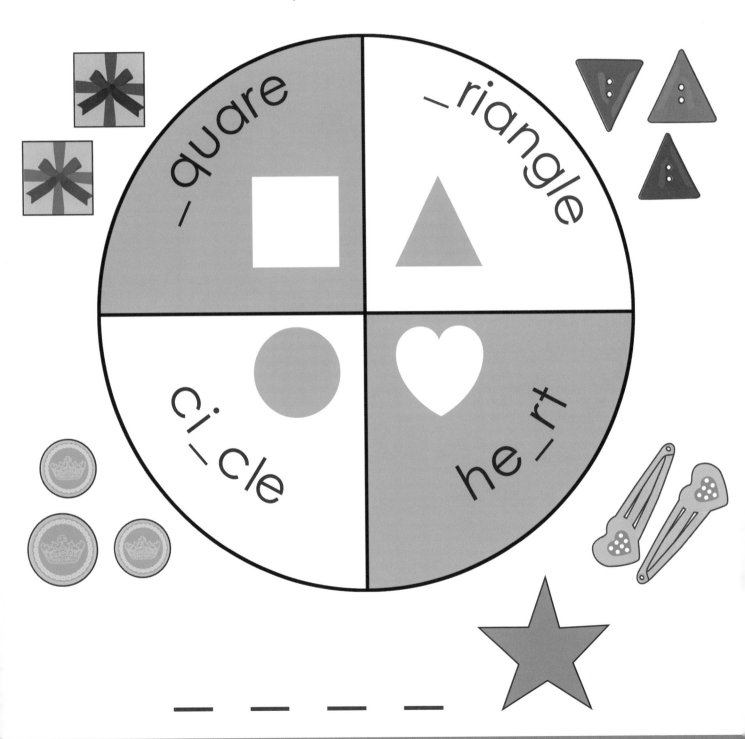

_ quare

_ riangle

ci_cle

he_rt

_ _ _ _ _

Which shape has three sides?

Bright colors

Trace over the color words, and then draw a line
to where they are on the rainbow.

yellow

green

purple

red

blue

orange

pink

What color am I?

What
color is
the shirt?

What
color is the
motorcycle?

What
color is the
strawberry?

_ _ _ _ _ _   _ _ _ _ _   _ _ _

Have you ever seen a rainbow in the sky?

On the farm

Draw a line between each farm animal and the noise it makes.

baa baa

quack

oink

cock-a-doodle-doo

naa naa

moo

Farm foods

Can you trace over the names of the foods we get from the farm?

eggs   cereal   cheese   milk

What color is the cheese?

Word search

Can you find the farm words in the word search?

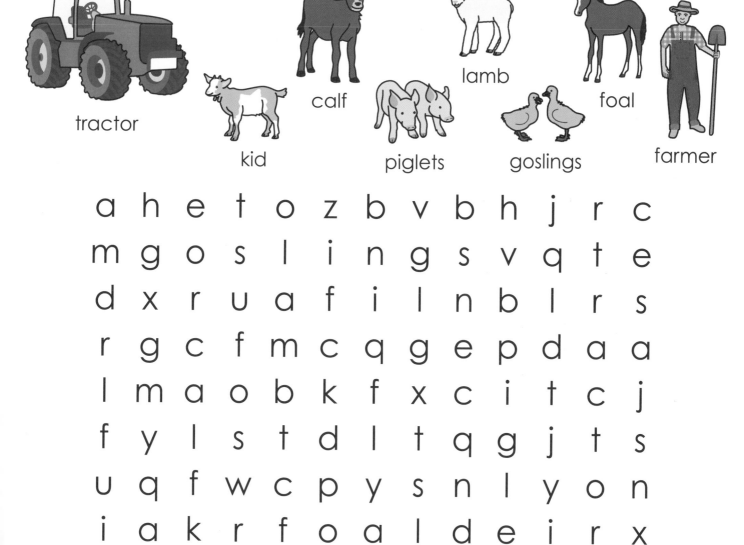

tractor

kid

calf

piglets

lamb

goslings

foal

farmer

a h e t o z b v b h j r c
m g o s l i n g s v q t e
d x r u a f i l n b l r s
r g c f m c q g e p d a a
l m a o b k f x c i t c j
f y l s t d l t q g j t s
u q f w c p y s n l y o n
i a k r f o a l d e i r x
p k u s u g v o m t x r k
w n f a r m e r v s j m g
b t h e p u a w i h k i d

A lamb is the baby of which wooly farm animal?

In the jungle

Fill in the letters to write the names of these jungle animals.

f_ _ g

ori _a

t_u_a_

_i_er

s_ _k_

Which jungle animal has a colorful beak?

Crossword

Use the picture clues to help you complete the wild animal crossword.

1 down

2 across

3 down

4 down

5 across

6 across

Which animal has a long, gray trunk?

Letter search

Can you find six things in this sea-life scene that begin with the letter "s"? Check the boxes when you find them.

seagull

sea horse

shark

shell

starfish

sun

Can you think of any other words that begin with the letter "s"?

Animal habitats

Using the word and picture clues, can you figure out what the four mixed-up animal names are? Write your answers in the spaces below.

I live in the desert   _ _ _ _ _ _   melca

I am from Africa   _ _ _ _ _   ebrza

I live in the ocean   _ _ _ _ _   hawel

I am from Australia   _ _ _   mue

At the poles

These animals live in cold climates. Can you trace over their names?

polar bear   walrus   penguins

How many tusks does the walrus have?

Creepy crawlies

Which two bugs do not begin with the letter "b"?

bee

caterpillar

butterfly

beetle

pill bug

Can you find the bug words in the word search?

ladybug

ant

worm

spider

b	q	s	l	t	d	m	l
v	a	n	t	w	s	z	a
k	r	c	g	e	p	j	d
b	f	h	i	d	i	m	y
w	o	r	m	p	d	r	b
i	a	o	c	l	e	o	u
n	g	s	k	j	r	f	g
a	p	f	r	n	t	e	z

Which bug's name begins with the letter "l"?

Letter match

Can you draw lines to match each pet to the first letter of its name?

m

c

t

g

r

p

d

k

Which pet has a hard shell?

First sounds

Draw a circle around the things that begin with the sounds below.

m

p

t

Which object is a musical instrument?

Foods we eat

Using the picture clues, can you work out
what the mixed-up food words are?

_ _ _ _ _ _ palpe

_ _ _ _ _ spae

_ _ _ _ _ _ niono

_ _ _ _ ikwi

Food groups

Draw a line between the foods on the
plate and their matching food group.

meat

dairy

grains

vegetables

fruits

Can you name the foods on the plate? Which do you like to eat?

Crossword

Use the picture clues to help you complete the seaside crossword.

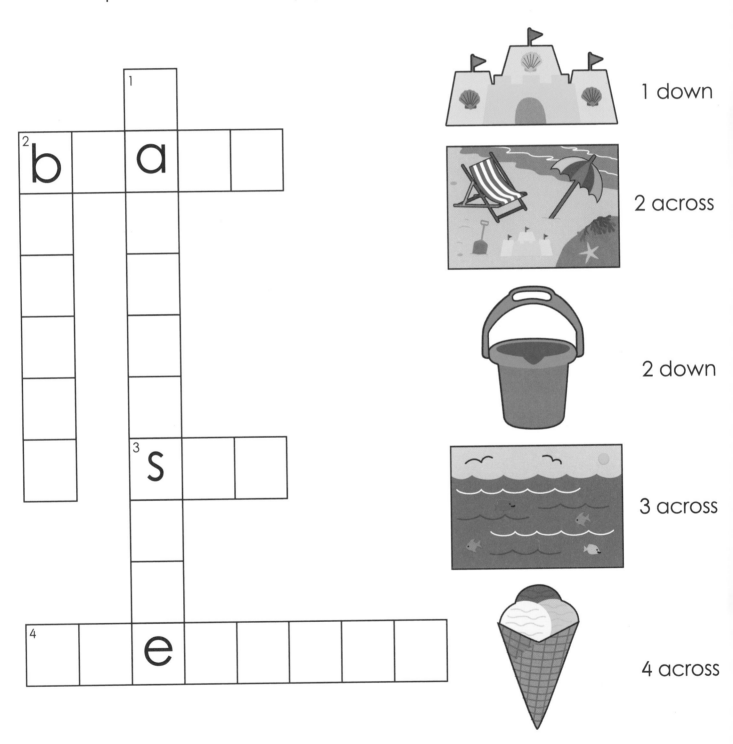

1 down

2 across

2 down

3 across

4 across

What do you like to do at the seaside?

Active fun

Trace over the names of the sports, and then draw lines to match the words to the pictures.

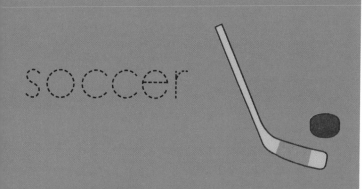

soccer

tennis

hockey

cycling

Can you find the activity words in the word search?

dancing

baseball

swimming

bowling

i	g	r	g	f	d	x	s
d	a	n	c	i	n	g	b
m	s	b	v	s	l	c	o
g	z	y	r	k	s	q	w
b	a	s	e	b	a	l	l
c	k	x	j	p	z	d	i
g	n	d	w	r	s	q	n
s	w	i	m	m	i	n	g

Which of the sports and hobbies is your favorite?

Outdoors

Trace over the names of some things you might find in the park.

bird   flower   pond   tree

Can you find three things in this shed scene that begin with the letter "w"? Check the boxes when you find them.

watering can
☐

wheelbarrow
☐

window
☐

What do you use a watering can for?

Color match

Draw a line between the household objects
and the color word they match.

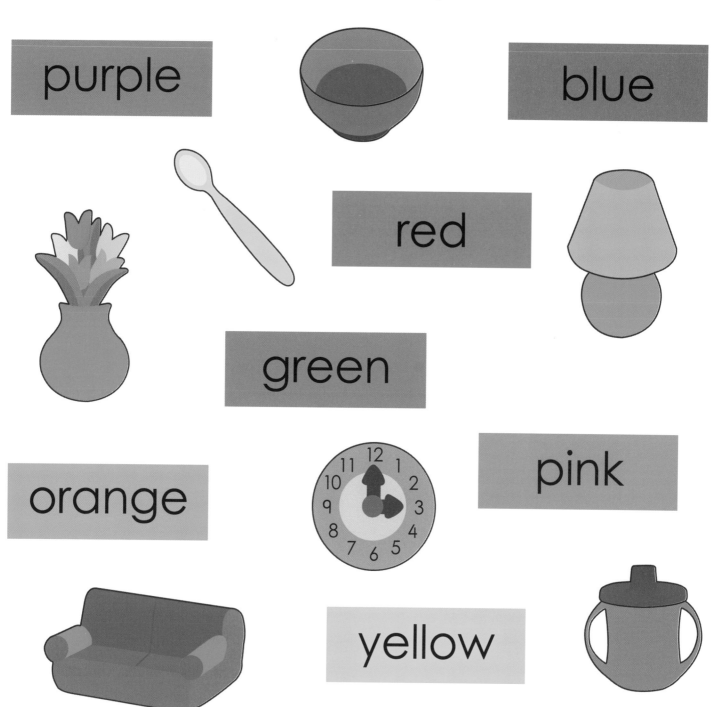

purple

blue

red

green

orange

pink

yellow

What time does the clock say?

Word search

Can you find these things you do at school in the word search?

math art reading music sports geography writing science

e h a r t g r m g k y t m
t b j p u r s p o r t s a
n v r i l e j s n l d i t
d g e o g r a p h y w s h
i p a j o z k c r k o h s
m a d q b g v s r y p a o
u x i x n w r i t i n g x
s u n s q t y u d k m c h
i a g z l i c t h b q w e
c j v b d m v o e c l u n
q a p m z s c i e n c e w

What is your favorite subject at school?

My toy box

Fill in the missing letters to complete the sentences.

My toy car has round	My teddy bear's fur is	My tricycle goes very

w _ e _ _ s   s _ _ t   _ a _ t

Toy puzzle

Using the word and picture clues, can you work out what the four mixed-up words are? Write your answers in the spaces below.

Makes lots of noise   _ _ _ _ _   udrm

Can fly very high   _ _ _ _ _   ietk

Has a pretty dress   _ _ _ _ _   lodl

Are very colorful   _ _ _ _ _ _ _   atnpis

Do you have any of these toys in your toy box?

Last sounds

Draw a line between each object and the letter that makes its last sound.

n

p

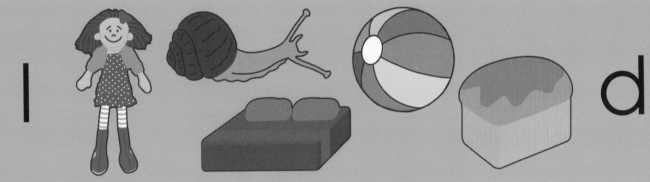

l

d

Missing sounds

Fill in the missing last sounds of the different clothes words.

shoe_   glov_   T-shir_   ha_

What is the last sound in your name?

Crossword

Use the picture clues to help you complete the horse crossword.

1 across

2 down

3 down

4 across

5 across

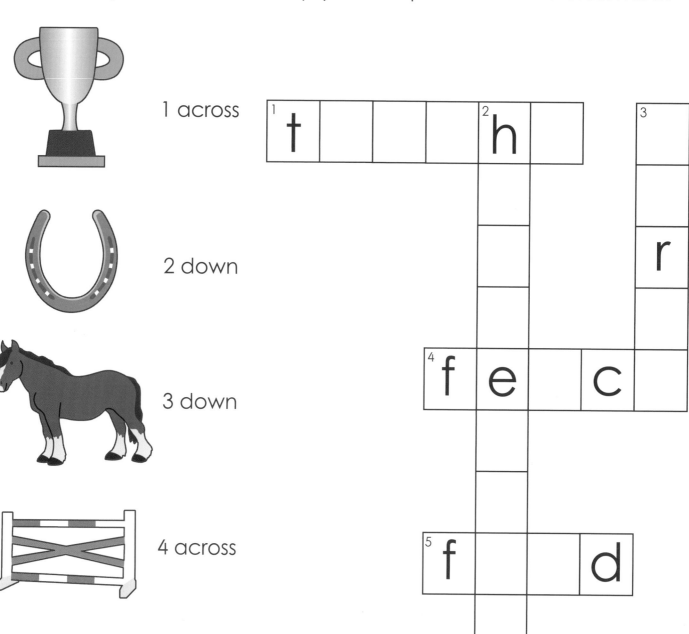

Have you ever been horse riding?

Word wheel

Fill in the missing letters of the words on the wheel.
Use these letters to spell the name of the vehicle below.

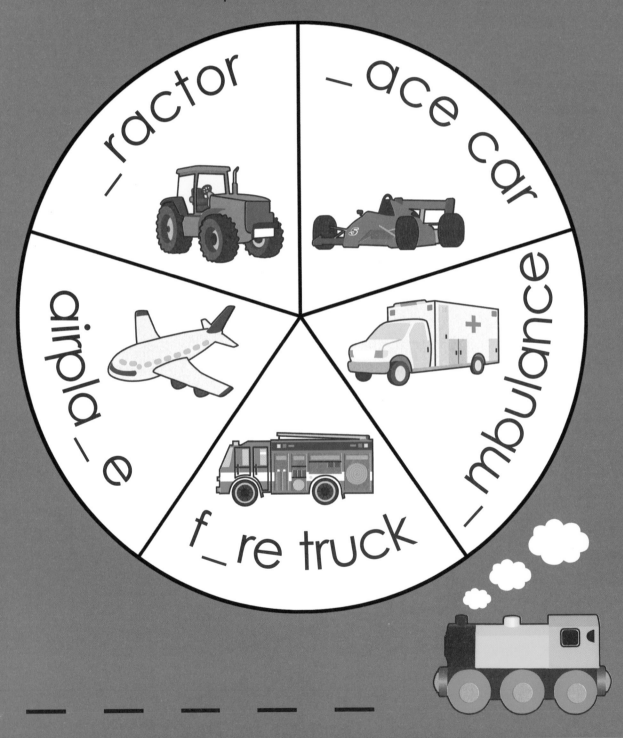

_ractor

_ace car

airpla_e

f_re truck

_mbulance

_ _ _ _ _ _

Which of these vehicles can fly?

Busy machines

Trace over the names of the different machines.

police
car

cruise
ship

cement
mixer

space
shuttle

What do I drive?
Complete the sentences using the machine names above.

I race to
emergencies in a

I travel on
water in a

I work on the
construction site in a

Which machine flies into space?

Our Earth

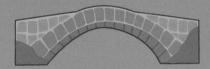

Unscramble the words to complete the sentences.

Bees collect nectar from flowers and make it into

nehoy

_ _ _ _ _

Trees are turned into

eppra

_ _ _ _ _

Cows eat grass to help them make

lkmi

_ _ _ _

Draw lines to match the natural materials to some of the things they are made into.

rocks

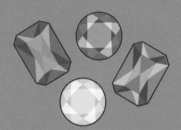

metals

precious stones

oil

Do you know any other materials we get from the earth?

Crossword

Use the picture clues to help you complete the space crossword.

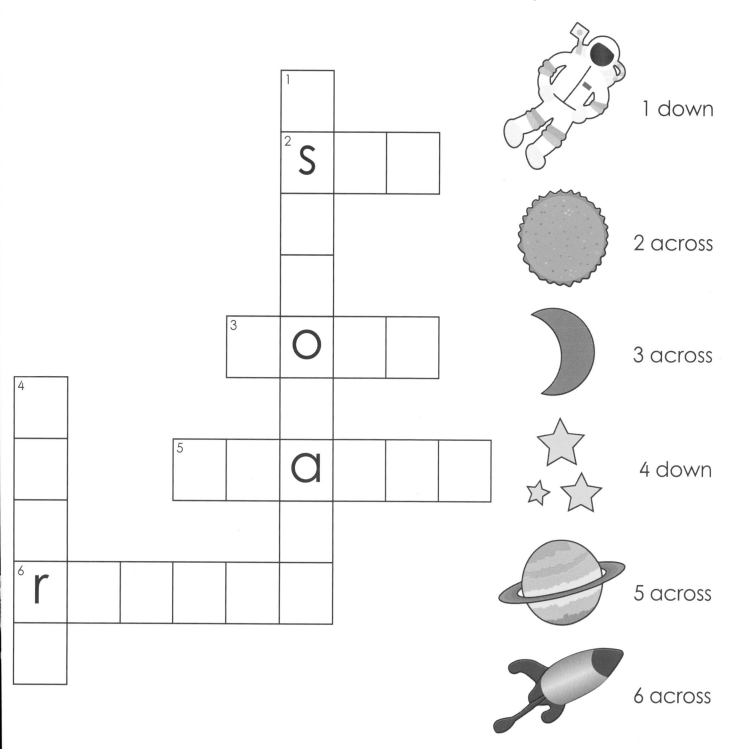

1 down

2 across

3 across

4 down

5 across

6 across

Which of the space things begins with the letter "r"?

Rhyme time

Draw lines between each
of the rhyming pairs.

man

hen

frog

map

dog

can

cap

pen

Odd one out

Trace over the words and circle the one that
doesn't rhyme with the others.

cat

hat

fish

bat

Do you know any other rhyming pairs?

Missing letters

Complete the dinosaur sentences by filling in the missing letters. The pictures will help you.

Triceratops has three pointed

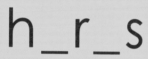
h _ r _ s

On its feet, Iguanodon has two big

c _ a w _

Stegosaurus's tail has

s _ i _ e _

Baryonyx has very sharp

_ e _ t _

Which dinosaur is your favorite?

Word search

Can you find the pirate words in the word search?

a w i d z h o o k p n d o
h y s l i e j n x o g s t
e p a r r o t x e g t v v
o i r g i w d r c o k x p
e r p m c r s i n u c j t
y a n w t y h b a j k e d
d t h s p m i l q w p u l
z e b e y e p a t c h r a
s q c a v a r z y u j v h
k c l z q h t m v b g b a
b c u t l a s s h k q x t

pirate

hat

ship

cutlass

eye patch

hook

parrot

What color are the parrot's feathers?

Princess puzzles

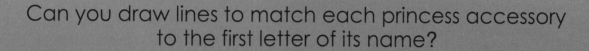

Can you draw lines to match each princess accessory
to the first letter of its name?

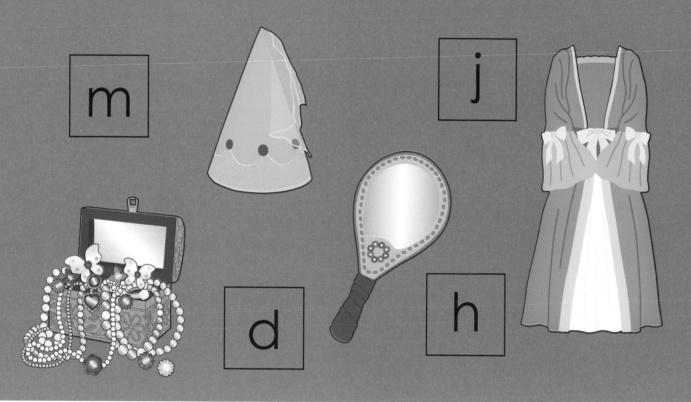

m

j

d

h

At the palace
Trace over the princess words below.

castle   wand   tiara   princess

How many jewels are on the tiara?

Create your own